SWIM FOR YOUR LIFE!

Stewart Ross

Timeliners

CONTENTS

TO THE READER

Swim for your Life! is set in Mesopotamia over 4,000 years ago. It takes place among the Sumerians, an ancient people who developed one of the earliest civilisations. The laws, the places and some of the characters really existed. Other things, such as the children and their adventures, I made up to bring to life one of the most important periods in the history of the world.

Stewart Ross

THE STORY SO FAR

THE BEGINNING OF CIVILISATION

For most of their time on Earth, human beings were nomads – they did not have permanent homes, but moved around in search of food. They hunted animals and gathered fruits, nuts and shellfish, like oysters.

Then, some 12,000 years ago, people in some parts of the world settled down and became farmers. They built villages and looked after their crops and animals. As not everyone was needed to work on the land, different jobs developed. While most people were farmers, others were soldiers, merchants, priests and rulers. The unfortunate ones were slaves.

Villages grew into towns, and some of the towns into cities defended by high walls. This was the beginning of civilisation.

***

The Sumerian civilisation was one of the very first, dating as far back as 6500 BCE. It grew up in an area known as Mesopotamia, around the great Tigris and Euphrates rivers. Today this region lies in the country of Iraq.

The Sumerians made several inventions. Two of the most significant were the wheel and writing. They did not have paper but wrote by scratching wedge-shaped marks on wet clay with a reed. In this way, they kept business records, set down the law, and even told stories.

The earliest written laws we have discovered were set out by King Ur-Nammu in about 2100 BCE. There were 57 laws in all, but only around 30 of them have survived. The story that follows shows just how important those written laws were.

TIME LINE

BCE (Before Common Era)
('c.' means 'about')

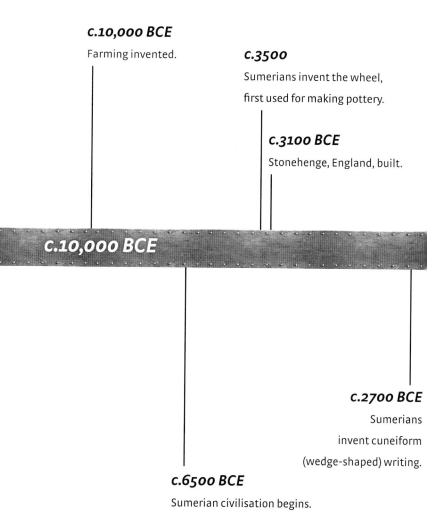

c.10,000 BCE
Farming invented.

c.3500
Sumerians invent the wheel,
first used for making pottery.

c.3100 BCE
Stonehenge, England, built.

c.10,000 BCE

c.2700 BCE
Sumerians
invent cuneiform
(wedge-shaped) writing.

c.6500 BCE
Sumerian civilisation begins.

Romans begin conquest of Mesopotamia.

c.1696–1654 BCE

King Hammurabi of Babylon rules over
Mesopotamia.

c.2580 BCE

Great Pyramid of Giza, Egypt, built.

115 CE

c.1940 BCE

City of Ur attacked, and
Sumerians conquered by
the Amorites.

c.2029–1982 BCE

Reign of King Shulgi, son of
Ur-Nammu. Ziggurat of Ur finished.

c.2047–2029 BCE

Reign of King Ur-Nammu in Sumer.

Chapter 1

BET YOU CAN'T!

It was Lagasha's idea. 'Come on, Meslim,' she said, glancing around to make sure no one was looking. 'Let's go for a swim.'

It's not easy to say no to your big sister, especially when it's someone as bossy as Lagasha. Besides, it was really hot and the blue-grey waters of the River Euphrates looked so inviting.

But our parents had forbidden us to go swimming on our own. It was too dangerous, Father warned. The currents were stronger than they looked, and every year children were swept away and never seen again. Rumour said they ended up downstream as slaves.

I hesitated. 'I'm not sure, Lagasha,' I muttered. 'We're supposed to be looking after the fields, stopping the birds from eating our wheat...'

My voice trailed off as she gave me one of her *you're-such-a-wimp* looks. 'Don't be pathetic, Meslim,' she said, rolling her eyes. 'A quick dip won't do any harm. It'll help us with all that boring bird scaring, too: stop us going to sleep.'

I felt a drip of sweat trickling down the side of my nose. 'Oh, all right,' I replied, setting off towards the river. 'But only a quick dip.'

You can guess what happened, can't you? The day was so hot and the water so cool that our quick dip soon became a long, refreshing bathe.

At first, we played games, splashing in the shallows near the bank. Later, we dived down into the murky waters and tried to catch fish with our bare hands. We had no luck. Though they looked gormless, the fish were always too quick. They appeared not to notice as we edged up behind them. But when we made a grab, with a flick of the tail they were gone.

After a dozen failures, Lagasha came up to the surface, wiped the water from her eyes, and pointed to a sandbank near the middle of the stream. 'Bet you can't swim out there,' she said.

'You mean that island-thing? Of course I can!'

'Go on then, Meslim. Prove it!'

'Sure! I'll race you.'

I'll never know whether or not I could have won the bet. Long before either of us was even half way towards our target, something terrible happened.

Lagasha was a year older than me, taller and stronger. Not surprisingly, she was soon two lengths ahead and drawing further away with every stroke. I fixed my eyes on the splashing of her heels, and did my best to keep up. It was no good. I might reach the island, I realised, but I'd never win the race.

I shifted my gaze slightly to the left to check we were headed in the right direction. Hang on! Where was the island? It should be there, straight ahead. But no. Before me lay nothing but the broad, swift-flowing Euphrates. I craned my head round further – and saw the island far to my left.

That's when I realised. About twenty paces from the shore, no more than a quarter of the distance to the island, the river suddenly became deeper and much swifter. We were now in a powerful current, and with every stroke it carried us further and further downstream, away from the shore.

'Lagasha!' I screamed. 'Lagasha! Come back! Look where you are!'

She obviously couldn't hear me because she continued swimming as strongly as ever. As I watched, horrified, Father's ominous warning echoed through my mind: *Every year children are swept away by the current and never seen again*

Chapter 2

THE SHADOW

Lagasha might not have heard my words, but someone else did. Father. My feeble cries were drowned out by a mighty roaring from the river bank.

'Lagasha! Listen to me!' boomed a voice that sounded more like an ox than a human. 'Turn round and swim in this direction.'

Ahead of me, I saw my sister pause and look over her shoulder. Her smile soured to a look of terror as she realised what was happening.

'Help!' she yelled. 'Father! Meslim! Help me! The current's dragging me away!'

Once again Father's voice roared over the waters. 'Don't panic, Lagasha. Save your energy. I'm coming!'

I didn't know what frightened me more, the power of the current or the thought of Father coming into the water. If that sounds strange, let me explain.

Some years previously, my father had been badly injured. He had been burned down the left side of his body. His left arm was twisted and scarred, and his left leg hardly worked at all. When he walked, it dragged behind him in the dust like a sack. How would a man like that swim?

But swim he did. Pulling his useless leg behind him, he limped down the bank until he was level with

Lagasha, then plunged into the water and struck out towards his daughter.

At first, where there was almost no current, he made good progress. Then the full force of the stream hit him and, despite his best efforts, he was carried away just as Lagasha had been. Before long, both he and my sister were out of sight.

And what of me all this time? Luckily, I had not been carried out so far into the stream and slowly, stroke by stroke, I was able to edge back towards the bank. But I was dreadfully tired. My arms felt as if they were made of bronze and I could hardly kick my legs. When I opened my mouth to breathe, instead of air, my mouth filled with water. I coughed, and my head sank beneath the surface.

At that moment, a powerful hand closed around my arm. Half-conscious, I felt myself pulled steadily towards the bank by a swimmer whose strong, steady strokes I knew only too well. It was Mother.

Before long, my feet touched the bottom and I stood up, crying with relief, shame and anxiety. Once I was on dry land, Mother told me to stay where I was while she ran off downstream in the direction Father had taken.

As I sat there, feeling more and more wretched, my little brother and sisters came up and asked what was going on. I did my best to explain. The four of us then waited in silence, staring down the river, hoping and praying that Lagasha and Father had made it safely to the bank.

When we saw them coming towards us, we jumped to our feet and ran to meet them. Mother's lovely face shone with relief, but Father and Lagasha were almost too exhausted to speak. As we reached them, they slumped down on the ground and closed their eyes.

'Now children,' said Mother, 'let this be a lesson to all of you...'

She paused and looked up. As she did so, a dark shadow fell across her brow. We were not alone.

Chapter 3

KU-BAU

The shadow that fell across Mother's face was a man's. I sensed, even without looking at him, who it was. I had known Ku-Bau all my life, and I had never liked him. Tall, with eyes set close together over a beak-like nose, he reminded me of a bird of prey, a vulture hovering over its victim.

'Well done, Dumazid,' he said, staring hard at Father. 'I was watching from that hill over there and I saw everything. How clever to think of using your magic to rescue your daughter.'

Father frowned. 'What did you say, Ku-Bau?'

'Still got water in your ears, have you? Well, let me explain. Everyone knows about your evil ways, Dumazid. They only have to look at you to see you're no good – the limping sorcerer, they call you. Did you know that?'

Father clenched his fists but said nothing.

'Well, the time has come to put a stop to your tricks, Dumazid. This time you've picked on someone who's not going to take your wickedness lying down.'

'I haven't a clue what you're talking about, Ku-Bau,' said Father, shaking his head. 'What's all this nonsense about "wickedness" and "evil ways"? You must have dreamed it up after you'd drunk too much beer.'

The remark brought a blush of anger to Ku-Bau's lean cheek. 'You'll regret that remark,' he sneered. 'And so will you, children,' he continued, staring hard at each of us in turn.

He turned his gaze on Mother. 'As for you, Gadia,' he said, giving her a mean attempt at a smile, 'you made a terrible mistake, didn't you? But it's not too late. I'll get you back, just you see if I don't.'

Father's patience finally snapped. 'Be quiet, Ku-Bau,' he barked. 'How dare you threaten me and scare my family! Just when we've all had a terrible shock, too. Now leave us alone! Go away!'

Ku-Bau gave another of his thin, cruel smiles. 'Yes, I'll go, Dumazid, and leave you to get over your shock. But I warn you, there's a much bigger shock coming your way very soon. And this time there won't be a happy ending. Not for you, anyway.'

With that, he turned away and strode off through the fields.

'What on earth was all that about?' asked Mother, gathering us about her and starting back towards our house.

Father shrugged. 'Goodness only knows. He doesn't like me, and I expect he's looking for someone to blame for all the things that have been going wrong on his farm.'

'What things?' I asked.

'He's had a bit of bad luck, Meslin. His wheat crop has been poor for the last two years, and some of his pigs and oxen have died. It's probably because he spends more time drinking beer than looking after his farm, but he doesn't see that. He has to blame someone, and that someone is me.'

'But it's not serious, is it?' asked Lagasha, who had recovered some of her energy after the peril of the river.

Father turned to her. 'No, not serious, my girl. But something else is. What on earth did you think you were doing disobeying me and going into the river on your own? And taking Meslim with you!'

'I'm sorry, Father…'

'Sorry? I should hope so. When we get back home, you and your brother will find out just how angry I am!'

We never did find out. On reaching our house, we found the front door blocked by two soldiers in the uniform of Prince Shulgi.

'Dumazid, you're under arrest,' said the broader of the two men.

'Eh? What for?'

'Working with the evil demon Lamashtu to harm your neighbours and their animals.'

Chapter 4

DUMAZID THE LIMPER

Before I go on, I think I'd better explain a few things. My family and Ku-Bau's, both Sumer people, had lived near each other for generations. Both farmed land beside the great River Euphrates, not far from the mighty city of Ur. When they were young, Ku-Bau and my father, Dumazid, were good friends. They helped each other in the fields and went fishing together in the river.

Ku-Bau's family was better off than ours. They had more land, raised more animals, and kept many more slaves. They were magistrates, too: it was their job to see that the law was obeyed. Their house, with its shady pools and quiet gardens, was one of the finest in the district.

It was to this house that Ku-Bau brought his young bride, Etani. He had married her, said the gossips, because of her wealth.

One evening, as father was walking by Ku-Bau's house on his way back from the fields, he noticed smoke pouring from a window. The place was on fire! Moments later, Ku-Bau and his household hurried outside, shouting and pointing at the angry red-orange flames licking at the roof timbers. Two women were trapped inside, they said, the master's wife, Etani, and Gadia, the loveliest of her slaves.

Ku-Bau stood still as a stela – frozen like a stone – too frightened to act. But not Father. Careless of his own safety, he plunged into a pool to dampen his clothing then rushed into the burning building. With his bare hands he wrenched open the smouldering door to Etani's rooms, freeing her and the slave Gadia. The two ran to safety. But as Father was following them out, part of the roof collapsed and a huge timber crashed down on his left shoulder. His arm was dislocated, his leg broken in three places, and the whole left side of his body, including his face, hideously burned.

For several days it looked as if Father would die. His life was saved by the tender nursing of Gadia. For three weeks she never left his bedside. She cared for him like a child, anointing his burns with oil, changing his bandages, and feeding him a soup she had made herself.

When Father was well enough to return to his own home, Ku-Bau asked him what he would like as a reward for saving his wife.

Without a moment's hesitation, Father replied, 'I would dearly like the hand in marriage of Gadia, your slave girl.'

'Marry a slave girl!' spluttered Ku-Bau. 'Are you out of your mind?'

'No,' replied Father calmly. 'I have learned that she is not only lovely, but also wise and kind and capable. I love her and she loves me. When she comes to my house, I will set her free and we will marry.'

And so they did, and their lives became one of the most famous love stories in all Ur.

But Ku-Bau did not share the people's joy. Although married, he had had his own eye on the pretty slave girl. He had planned to divorce Etani, with whom he had no children, and take Gadia for himself. Now this was no longer possible, he seethed with angry jealousy.

As the friendship between Ku-Bau and Father ended, Ku-Bau's life began to fall apart. He spent a fortune rebuilding his house larger and grander than before. He threw parties, drank too much beer, and neglected his farm. Month by month, year by year, his dislike of Father spread through his mind like a bed of nettles. He burned with a bitter hatred for the man he blamed for stealing his happiness and ruining his life.

That is why he had gone to the palace of Prince Shulgi and demanded that his neighbour, the man he called 'Dumazid the Limper', be arrested and charged with sorcery.

Chapter 5

THE LAW OF UR-NAMMU

We stood and watched in horror as the soldiers tied Father's arms behind his back. He did not resist, saying we were not to worry because there had obviously been some mistake. He would come straight home as soon as he had explained things to Prince Shulgi.

'Don't think you'll be doing that, Dumazid,' growled the elder of the two soldiers as he knotted the ropes around Father's wrists.

'Why not?'

'Because we're not taking you to the Prince.'

A note of anxiety came into Father's voice. 'So where are you taking me?'

'To the magistrate.'

'The magistrate? But that's Ku-Bau, and he doesn't like me. In fact, he hates me! You can't take me to him. I demand to see Prince Shulgi!'

'Sorry sir. You can demand all you want, but the Prince himself said the magistrate should deal with this case.'

'He told you that, to your face?'

'He did, sir.'

With that, the soldiers tied a second rope round Father's neck and led him away up the dusty path towards Ku-Bau's house, about a thousand paces away.

As we watched him go, Mother called us to her and said in a quiet, determined voice, 'We must be strong, children. It's just a misunderstanding and I'm sure it will be sorted out in no time. Your father will probably be back with us later this evening.'

But Father did not return. When it grew dark, we huddled together and prayed to the great god Utu, the Lord of Truth. Please, we begged, open the eyes of Ku-Bau and show him that our father is no sorcerer but an honest farmer.

'Tomorrow, O Utu,' Mother chanted, 'when you rise from the mountains of the east, my two elder children will come to your temple in the city of Ur and offer you the richest gifts in our possession. Accept them, we pray, O Lord of Truth, for we need your justice.'

The three younger children and Lagasha and I were exhausted by the adventures of the day, and we fell asleep almost before the words were out of Mother's mouth. But, judging by the dark rings under her eyes the next morning, I don't think she slept much that night.

We woke at dawn. After a quick breakfast of bread and beans, we selected our three best chickens, killed them, and wrapped them in leaves as a present for the Lord of Truth. After a quick goodbye, Lagasha and I set out on the road for Ur. As she said, it was a rather different and much more serious adventure than that of the previous day.

By noon, we were in the heart of the city. Although I had been into Ur several times before, the place always amazed me. So many people! All those grand buildings! And looming over them all, the towering ziggurat built by King Ur-Nammu in honour of Nanna, the Moon God. Standing before it, I felt very small indeed.

We presented our chickens at the temple of the great god Utu. Afterwards, feeling hungry, we bought bread from a stall near the ziggurat. As we were eating it, I noticed a large clay tablet set up where everyone could see it. On its surface were strange marks.

'What's that, Lagasha?' I asked.

She frowned. 'Not sure, Meslim. It might be the law, set out in writing.'

'Writing? Is that those weird marks?'

'Yes, I think so.'

We were interrupted by a priest who was passing and overheard our conversation. 'Yes, children,' he said, speaking in a rather posh accent. 'That is the law given to us by His Majesty Ur-Nammu.'

Lagasha thanked him and asked a question that almost certainly saved Father's life. 'Please, sir, what does the law say about sorcerers?'

Chapter 6

THE PRINCE

The priest pointed to a row of marks on the tablet. 'This is what the law of Ur-Nammu says about sorcery, young lady,' he said pompously.

'Er, thank you, sir,' said Lagasha, 'but could you possibly read it to us, please?'

The priest sighed. 'Listen, I am Tungana, a High Priest. I have more important things to do than talk with children.'

'Please, sir!'

'Very well. It says, *If someone is accused of being a sorcerer, they must be tested by the water. If the water shows them to be innocent, the person who accused them must pay three pieces of silver.*'

'*Tested by water* – what does that mean, sir?' I asked

Tungana scowled at me. 'Questions, questions, child! Really, I am not your schoolteacher and I am far too busy to wait around here any longer. If you want to know what the law means, why don't you go and ask Prince Shulgi himself?'

With that, the grumpy priest strode off into the crowd. His remark about going to ask the Prince was a joke, but Lagasha didn't see it that way. Hauling me behind her, she set off towards the palace of Prince

Shulgi. When we reached the guards at the entrance, she went straight up to them and said Tungana, the High Priest, had sent her to speak with the Prince. It was the truth, sort of, and the guards were so surprised that they let us in.

Shortly afterwards, we found ourselves standing in a large, open room with pillars round the outside and a fountain playing in the middle. I was peering into the pool at the foot of the fountain to see if there were any fish in it, when a voice boomed, 'His Royal Highness Prince Shulgi! Down!'

Lagasha and I threw ourselves face down on the tiled floor. 'Children?' said a deep voice. 'Who and why?'

'I believe they are the elder daughter and son of Dumazid, the man who has been accused of sorcery,' explained a courtier. 'It is said he works with the evil demon, Lamashtu.'

'I know the case,' replied the deep voice, which I now realised belonged to the Prince. 'It was brought by the magistrate, Ku-Bau. I told him to deal with it himself. So why are these children here?'

'Please sir, er, I mean Your Majesty,' began Lagasha, 'Ku-Bau hates our father. It won't be fair!'

'Not fair! Be careful what you say, child, or I will have you whipped for lying.'

'But she's right, Your Majesty,' I blurted out. 'Ku-Bau is unkind to our father. He calls him "Limper". Our mother used to be his slave and he wants her back...'

'Silence!' cut in the courtier. 'The mother's name is

Gadia, Your Majesty. You may remember the story.'

The Prince gave a low chuckle. 'Ah yes! We all know the story of the farmer and the slave girl. Thank you for reminding me. So you think Ku-Bau is accusing Dumazid falsely, do you?'

'Yes,' I whispered.

'Be quiet, boy,' snapped the Prince. 'I was not speaking to you. Nevertheless, this case interests me. I will visit these families and deal with it myself.'

Chapter 7

THE WATER WILL REVEAL THE TRUTH

Imagine the scene. Prince Shulgi, surrounded by courtiers and guards, was standing on a wooden platform on the bank of the River Euphrates. Before him, only a few paces apart, stood Father and Ku-Bau. The magistrate wore the robe of blue silk that he had inherited from his grandfather. Father wore his farmer's clothes, a clean white shirt and a knee-length kilt.

We stood in a large crowd of onlookers assembled ten paces behind the two men. The matter had aroused great interest in the district, and the spectators had come to see the Prince and hear what he had to say.

He began by asking Ku-Bau to state his case. The magistrate spoke well, explaining how his crops had been poor, six of his oxen had died, and, two years running, his sows had failed to deliver piglets.

'Worse still, Great Prince,' he said, 'my dear wife, whom I love more than my own life, has not given us any children. There can be only one cause of such misfortunes, My Lord. Sorcery – evil magic. Someone has summoned the dreaded demon Lamashtu to curse me.

'I say "someone", but we all know who that person is. It's Dumazid the Limper –'

'Be careful, Ku-Bau,' interrupted the Prince. '"Limper" is not Dumazid's proper name.'

'I beg your pardon, My Lord,' replied Ku-Bau. 'But he does limp. And his face has been made foul by fire. In fact, he looks rather like the partner of Lamashtu, the female devil whom he worships.

'And why, we ask, does this twisted cinder of a man hate me? The answer is simple. Because I am handsome and he is misshapen and ugly, because he is embarrassed that he married one of my slave women, and because this woman would now rather be with me than him!'

'Liar!' muttered Mother under her breath as a ripple of surprise ran through the crowd.

'Silence!' commanded the Prince. 'Now Dumazid, let me hear your side of the story.'

'I have little to say, Your Majesty,' began Father. 'I do not hate Ku-Bau and have never wanted to harm him. His misfortunes are of his own making, perhaps because he prefers to drink beer rather than look after his farm.

'He has accused me of sorcery for one reason only: he is jealous of my beautiful wife, Gadia, whom he wants for himself. He actually said as much when we met on the river bank a couple of days ago.'

'All lies!' yelled Ku-Bau. 'The fellow's a twisted, limping liar! You only have to look at him to realise –'

'Enough!' snapped the Prince. 'It's not for you or even for me to decide. The law is clear: the water of the great Euphrates, tears from the eyes of the Goddess Tiamat, will reveal the truth.

'Dumazid will be thrown into the river. If he drowns, the waters will have shown his guilt. If he survives, they will have shown his innocence. And if that is the case, Ku-Bau must pay him three pieces of silver. That is the law of my father, the great King Ur-Nammu.'

No sooner had he said this than Ku-Bau took a step forward and asked, 'Just thrown into the river, Your Majesty? Surely that is no test?'

The Prince looked down at him and nodded. 'I agree. So, as a magistrate Ku-Bau, what do you suggest?'

Ku-Bau's eyes narrowed. He cast a quick look towards Father and smiled. 'I believe a true test of guilt or innocence would be to swim right across the river, Your Majesty.'

The Prince thought for a moment. 'That's very hard,' he said. 'But I suppose it's fair. When Dumazid is thrown into the river, he must swim to the opposite bank. If he manages to do so, he will be innocent.'

Once more a ripple of conversation ran through the crowd. Swim across the Euphrates? Only the strongest swimmers could do that. A man with a crippled leg and a twisted arm didn't stand a chance.

He would surely drown.

Chapter 8

THE BATTLE OF BRITAIN

At the Prince's command, four of his guards took hold of Father's arms and legs and heaved him into the river. Just as Lagasha and I had done when we went swimming, he found it easy going near the bank where there was hardly any current. But gradually, as he moved further out, the water began to swirl in little waves around him and carry him further and further away from us.

Beside me, Mother was silently weeping. Her tears fell to the ground by my feet, making little craters in the dust. My younger brother and sisters were sobbing, too.

Trying my hardest not to cry myself, I took Lagasha's hand. 'Do you think we should pray?' I whispered.

'Yes, Meslim. Only the gods can help him now.'

'Who do we ask?'

'Only the mighty An, the Father of the Gods, can save him. We must ask for his help and his strength.'

I can't remember exactly what I said, but it was something like this:

'Great and holy An, please help my father Dumazid. He is a good, good man. He has to swim across the river to prove he is innocent. I know he is innocent, but one of his legs doesn't work properly and he will never make it to the other side without your strength. Please help him. Please!'

I repeated 'please' over and over again as I watched Father battle against the current. He was making almost no progress and his strokes were becoming weaker and weaker. I could imagine his bad leg dragging behind him in the water, pulling him back, pulling him down...

'Please, great An! Please help him!'

Father was little more than half way across. There, the current was at its strongest, and as we watched he grew smaller and smaller until he disappeared from view round a bend in the river. For a long time, the crowd remained silent. Then, with a cry, Mother fell to her knees and covered her face with her hands.

'My children!' she sobbed. 'What will become of us?'

Ku-Bau took a step towards her. 'Don't worry, my dearest Gadia. I'll take care of you,' he said. His greasy voice sounded like oil sliding into a jar.

Mother looked up in horror. 'Never, Ku-Bau! Never!'

'But think of your children, Gadia dear...'

He was cut short by Lagasha. 'Look,' she shouted. 'Over there, on the other bank!'

All eyes turned to where she was pointing. A man was staggering along the path beside the river. A tall man, a man with a limp...It was Father!

'Well,' said the Prince, coming down from his platform. 'I think the water has told us what we need to know. Dumazid is innocent.' He turned to the magistrate. 'And you, Ku-Bau, are a liar!

'As soon as we have sent a boat over to collect Dumazid, you must pay him the money you owe.'

'But I don't have it, Your Majesty!'

'Then I suggest – no, I order – that you give him your house instead. And you can have his. After what you have done, I think that's fair, don't you?'

Three years have passed since that day. As the Prince commanded, we live in the splendid house that had once belonged to Ku-Bau. He moved into ours, but didn't stay long. It was too small, he said, and he and his wife left the district. No one knows where they went, and nothing has been heard of them since.

Of course, after Ku-Bau's disappearance, the Prince needed a new magistrate. Who do you think he gave the job to? I'll give you one guess…

THE HISTORY FILE

THE CIVILISATION OF SUMER

Although the Sumer civilisation did not last long after the reign of King Shulgi, we are astonished by the many remarkable things it achieved all those years ago. Sumerians learned to irrigate their fields with water from the Rivers Tigris and Euphrates, and grew all kinds of cereals and other crops. They were also one of the first civilisations to brew beer.

They were great builders, digging canals, channels and ditches, and raising large brick structures, such as the Ziggurat of Ur. Other notable buildings were palaces and temples, sometimes with great domes of brick.

Educated Sumerians understood mathematics and how to use an abacus. They were some of the world's first astronomers, too, and made maps of the stars and planets.

Archaeologists have found objects and materials from far and wide in Sumerian settlements. We believe their traders exchanged goods with places as distant as Lebanon on the Mediterranean Sea and Mozambique off the coast of Africa. Skilled Sumerian craftworkers made decorated pots and charming jewellery from gold, silver and ivory.

The walls around Sumerian cities were not built for show. The cities of Mesopotamia were almost always at war with each other, and the Sumerians may have been the first civilisation to use professional soldiers. Men were armed with spears and shields (but not swords), and used four-wheeled battle chariots pulled by a type of donkey.

HOW DO WE KNOW?

How do we know so much about a people who lived over 4,000 years ago? Much of our evidence comes from objects, large and small, studied by archaeologists. We also have a remarkable box, known as the Standard of Ur, covered with mosaic images of life in Sumerian times. Above all, though, we learn about ancient Sumer from its writings.

THE DEVELOPMENT OF WRITING

The earliest form of writing was simply pictures: an outline of a bird, for example, or a wavy line to represent water. But some abstract things – like honour or truth – can't be easily illustrated in a picture. To represent such ideas, the Sumerians invented signs or symbols. Over time, these became a written language.

Some signs represented objects, others stood for sounds (vowels or syllables). Sumerian writers put them together to express ideas (like the law) and tell stories. Their writing-signs were wedge-shaped or 'cuneiform'. This comes from *Cuneus*, the Latin word for a wedge.

The Epic of Gilamesh, one of the world's first great stories, was written in cuneiform.

Scholars had known about Sumerian cuneiform writing for centuries. But only in the middle of the 19 century (1801-1900) did the scholars George Smith and Henry Rawlinson discover how to translate it. Once they had learned the secrets of cuneiform, the world of the Sumerians suddenly opened up.

After thousands of years, we were finally able to learn of the amazing ideas and achievements of a fascinating civilisation.

NEW WORDS

An
Sumerian sky god.

Anoint
To bless with holy oil.

Bronze
Hard mixture of copper and tin.

Cuneiform
Writing done with wedge-shaped symbols.

Euphrates
One of the large rivers running through Mesopotamia (modern-day Iraq).

Lamashtu
Female demon or monster.

Magistrate
Person responsible for seeing the law is obeyed.

Nomad
Person who moves from place to place, never settling.

Ox
Cow used for work, like pulling a cart.

Professional
Doing a job for money.

Sorcerer
Magician, often wicked.

Sow
Female pig.

Stela
Large carved stone.

Ur
Huge Sumerian city.

Utu
Sumerian sun god, associated with justice.

Ziggurat
Huge, pyramid-shaped brick temple on a platform.

TIMELINERS
BRING HISTORY ALIVE!

This series by Stewart Ross really sends the reader
back into history! Each exciting book brings the past alive
by linking key events to a fast-moving narrative.

978-1-78322-549-1

978-1-78322-559-0

978-1-78322-560-6

978-1-78322-547-7

978-1-78322-548-4

978-1-78322-567-5

978-1-78322-565-1

978-1-78322-566-8

978-1-78322-561-3

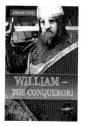

978-1-78322-537-8

978-1-78322-568-2

978-1-78322-592-7

978-1-78322-631-3

978-1-78322-644-3

978-1-78322-593-4

978-1-78322-632-0

978-1-78322-630-6

978-1-78322-643-6

978-1-78322-623-8

978-1-78322-624-5

978-1-78322-610-8